T0195902

The Spies at Carpenters' Hall

A Blueprint for a Revolution

by Charles and Nancy Cook

authorHOUSE®

AuthorHouse™
1663 Liberty Drive
Bloomington, IN 47403
www.authorhouse.com
Phone: 1 (800) 839-8640

Published by AuthorHouse 01/10/2020

ISBN: 978-1-7283-4059-3 (sc)
ISBN: 978-1-7283-4058-6 (e)

Library of Congress Control Number: 2019920825

Print information available on the last page.

This book is printed on acid-free paper.

This Book is dedicated to the members of the Carpenters' Company and to all who visit Carpenters' Hall with a belief that each individual contributes to the whole, and the efforts of every one of us make a difference.

CHAPTER ONE

Hide not your talents, they for use were
made: What's a sun-dial in the shade?

Poor Richard's Almanack
By Benjamin Franklin

*F*rancis Daymon was a librarian. He liked books. He liked people. He had read many great stories about many great people, but he never imagined that one day he, Francis Daymon, would play an essential part in one of the most important events in world history.

He could not imagine his own importance, because he thought great events were the result of brave and glorious acts. Great leaders made speeches, led armies, and were cheered by crowds. How was it possible he could ever do something important—something that would change the world forever!

Francis Daymon was on the second floor of Carpenters' Hall. Carpenters' Hall had been built between 1770 and 1773 by members of the Carpenters' Company, a trade guild operating in Philadelphia. Trade guilds began in Europe and dated back centuries. Merchants and craft workers formed guilds to teach new, younger members how to perform the work the guild claimed for their own. There were many types of guilds, such as barbers, bakers, and barrel makers called coopers. There were craft guilds that constructed all the buildings, including two of the most powerful guilds—the masons and the carpenters.

The Carpenters' Company had built their own building in Philadelphia. The building—Carpenters' Hall-- was used for meetings by the Company and rented out for other gatherings. So, it was on the second floor of Carpenters' Hall that Daymon's employer, Benjamin Franklin, had arranged to begin a lending library. It was the first free library system in America. Books were very expensive. They could cost as much as a month's wages for the average worker, so they just were seldom bought, but Benjamin Franklin knew how important learning from books could be. In his free library all the books—the great works by all the great writers—were made available so people could borrow and read them. When they returned a book they could borrow another. Franklin believed what the English philosopher Francis Bacon had said— "Knowledge is Power!" He wanted the American people to be knowledgeable. Benjamin Franklin knew the time was coming when this would be very important.

Francis Daymon was putting books that had been returned back on the shelves of the library. As he did so, Daymon thought how Franklin was an important leader. He was someone who would be written about in books. Benjamin Franklin was a great scientist, inventor, printer, and scholar. He had invented the **lightning rod**, the **"Franklin" stove**, and **bifocal glasses**. He was the first scientist to study the movement of the **Gulf Stream**. He favored **daylight savings** time in the summer. He improved the postal service and started the University of Pennsylvania, and also the first hospital in the colonies.

Daymon had one more book to return to the shelf when he happened to look out the northeast window of the library. There was Ben Franklin, himself, walking up the alley to Carpenters' Hall.

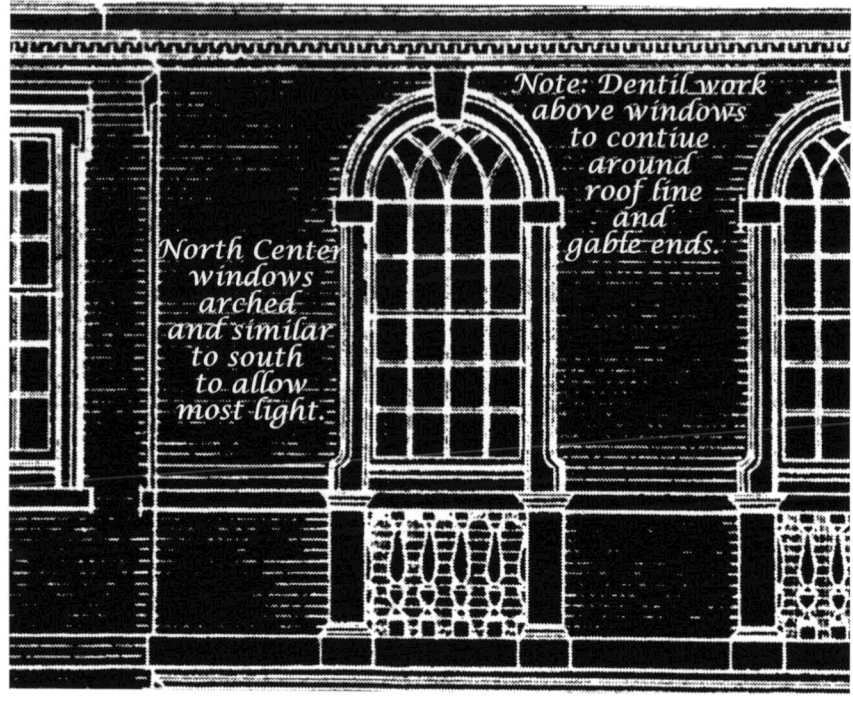

North Center Windows

This is the window from which Daymon looked out and saw Benjamin Franklin approaching the Hall. Even though windows and doors are good things to have in a wall, they actually stress and weaken the wall at each opening. A good builder has to make sure the walls are strong enough for each window and door. Otherwise, the wall would crack and fall apart. Benjamin Franklin was not concerned about the Carpenters' Company walls as he walked up to the Hall. He was thinking of the colonies, and if they would be strong enough not to crack or fall apart under stress.

There would be time to finish his restacking chores later. Daymon had something important he wanted to tell Benjamin Franklin, so he put the book back on his table and rushed down the stairs to wait for his employer at the front door.

The book that Daymon had not yet replaced was by the English poet John Milton. It contained several of his works, including the epic poem, *Paradise Lost* about the triumph of good over evil. There were other works by Milton in the book, including one entitled, "On His Blindness." The book fell open to one well-read passage that concluded—

"He also serves who only stands and waits."

CHAPTER TWO

The doors of wisdom are never shut.

Poor Richard's Almanack
By Benjamin Franklin

When Daymon saw him from the library's north window, Benjamin Franklin was coming from his home, less than a block away from Carpenters' Hall, across Chestnut Street. Just up Chestnut Street was the State House, where, it could not be known to Franklin or anyone yet, representatives of the colonies would meet and eventually declare the thirteen colonies of America free and independent of England. That would happen in less than seven months, in July of 1776.

At this time Benjamin Franklin was distressed, as he had been for some time. He had recently returned from England where he had met with many leaders of the British government in hopes of preventing war between the American colonies and England—the motherland. He had failed. He returned by ship to America, and throughout the long passage over the cold rolling waves of the Atlantic he worried and pondered the fate of the American colonies. He knew peace with England was impossible. A great war was now inevitable.

The colonists no longer felt obligated to England. The problems they faced in the New World required special attention that the English government did not have the time or the desire to give America. Since there was a great deal of opportunity available in America, the colonists were ready to accept responsibility for their own government rather than see England benefit from the efforts and risks they were taking.

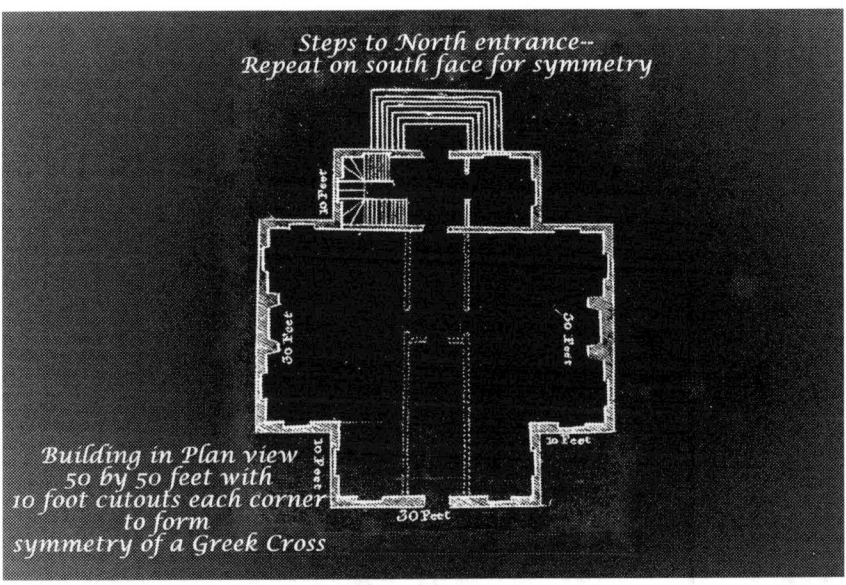

Building in Plan View

Carpenters' Hall is one of America's finest examples of balance and symmetry that characterizes **Georgian architecture**, but Benjamin Franklin thought that something else might be out of balance in the colonies. What if more Americans wanted to stay loyal than wanted to separate from England?

In the cold December wind of 1775, Franklin hunched over and walked with his head bent away from the wind. Momentarily he looked up as he was walking toward Carpenters' Hall. It was truly an impressive structure—one of his favorites. The balanced design characteristic of Georgian architecture was nicely done in this two-story brick building topped by a center **cupola**. From the central structure the building projected in four directions, creating a balanced **Greek cross plan** to the building. The bricks had been set in the stylish **Flemish bond** with dark glazed headers, which were bricks set with an end rather than a side facing out. This produced a stronger construction, but was also more expensive.

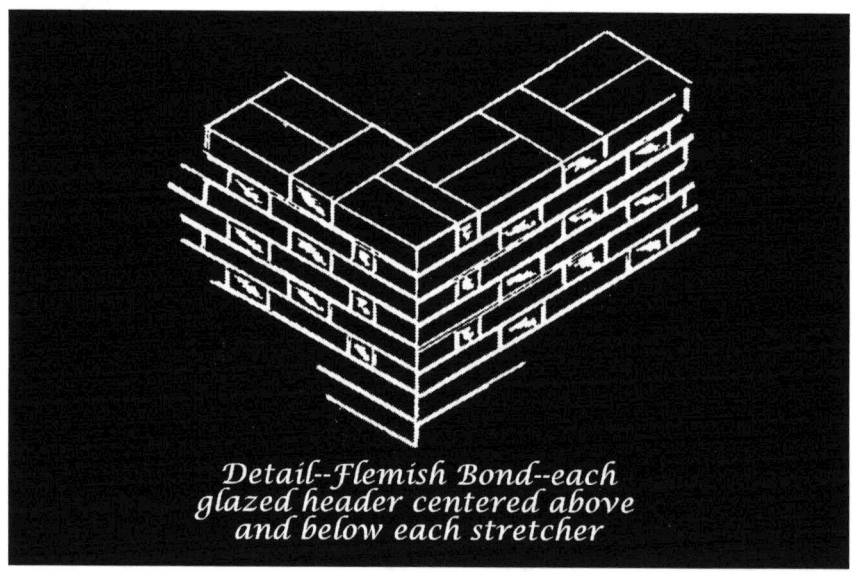

Detail--Flemish Bond--each glazed header centered above and below each stretcher

Detail—Flemish Bond

The Flemish bond was more expensive because it took longer to build, but it produced a stronger wall. Benjamin Franklin knew the colonies would need a strong **ally** to join them in a war against England, but that would also take time to build such an **alliance**.

The building was not yet complete. A new set of front doors would be installed, and additional work on the windows would be done, but the Carpenters' Company had indeed constructed a masterpiece—a way to show their craft and talents to others.

While Benjamin Franklin had been in England, the Carpenters' Company had made the hall available to the delegates of the colonies meeting in Philadelphia as the First Continental Congress.

Now many of the delegates had returned home. Through the postal system that Franklin had established everyone would be kept informed of developments. In fact, it was just a few days earlier that Benjamin Franklin and four others had been named to a very important committee of the Continental Congress. The four were to serve on the Committee of Secret Correspondence. As the first Post Master General of the colonies, Benjamin Franklin's involvement in a committee for corresponding seemed obvious, but this was secret correspondence. Today, we would call this work espionage and Benjamin Franklin and the others, spies.

They hang spies if they are caught.

Benjamin Franklin knew he could be in great danger if his intentions were ever discovered. This danger, however, was not what distressed Franklin. What caused him to worry was that he had no idea where, or how, or to whom to turn for help. He knew the American colonies would need foreign allies, but how was he to find another country to help America win a war of independence from England? England was, after all, considered the most powerful nation on earth with a large army and a great navy.

Benjamin Franklin hoped perhaps the Netherlands would offer assistance. The Dutch were great seafarers with exceptional trading interests throughout the world. Certainly, America represented almost unlimited trade possibilities for the Netherlands. Still, Franklin was not sure they would or could help.

He was indeed distressed. Where would he find an ally for America? The task was formidable. He was not sure where to look. With heavy thoughts, he started up the stone steps of Carpenters' Hall and looked up to see Francis Daymon at the door, holding it open for him.

CHAPTER THREE

Three may keep a secret, if two of them are dead.

Poor Richard's Almanack
By Benjamin Franklin

*F*rancis Daymon had something very important to tell Ben Franklin, and as soon as he began speaking his employer, Benjamin Franklin, was very interested to hear everything he had to say. Daymon had been contacted by a most unusual traveler from France.

Benjamin Franklin took a brief look around to be sure no one could over hear their conversation and then pulled Francis Daymon closer to him after the door had been closed.

He spoke to Francis in a whisper, "Now tell me from the beginning all you know about this fellow."

Francis Daymon proceeded to tell Franklin about the mysterious traveler whose full name and title was Chevalier Julien Alexandre Achard de Bonvouloir. He had been a French soldier several years before and may have been wounded in his leg. He walked with a limp and did have some trouble getting around even though he was not yet thirty. A few years earlier, Bonvouloir had sailed to America and toured the colonies. His knowledge of America had made him a valuable candidate to undertake the mission for which the King of France needed him.

Bonvouloir had been asked by an influential member of the French court to return to America. Since he had already been to America, he would have some existing contacts he could trust. This time rather than travel the colonies as a tourist, he was to return on a secret mission—as a spy, or, as he preferred to think of himself, as an ambassador to the American colonies.

The French were apparently very pleased that Bonvouloir had accepted this dangerous mission. He came from a distinguished family, and to find someone in France familiar with the British colonies was very rare. Still, the mission was so dangerous that Bonvouloir was on his own. If he got into any trouble, the French government would not help. They would deny any knowledge of him, his trip, or his mission. Even though he was on a mission for the King of France, he was not allowed to carry anything in writing confirming that he was sent by the King, himself.

At the same time, the King wanted Bonvouloir to obtain as much secret intelligence about the colonies as possible. He was also to advise the leaders of the colonies that if they were interested in overthrowing the existing English rule, the French would be quite willing to help them.

Franklin had many questions. The first was why would anyone want to come to America from France on such a dangerous mission?

Francis Daymon could not answer this question for sure, but Bonvouloir had told him in confidence that he was only being paid a couple hundred livres, barely enough to live on in Paris. Obviously, it was not for the money, but Bonvouloir was proud to be given an opportunity to do something for his country and perhaps gain the respect of the other distinguished members of his family.

Ben Franklin was not convinced. It was possible that this French fellow was part of a trap. Could he be a double agent, actually working for the British? Had he been sent to America to catch Franklin and others in their conspiracy against English rule?

Cupola

Publisher of Poor Richard's Almanack, Ben Franklin was one of America's first weather forecasters, but for more than the weather, he was interested in knowing "**which way the wind blows**.".

Was it possible Bonvouloir was actually working for King George? Benjamin Franklin had both great hopes and great concerns as he listened further to his librarian.

Francis Daymon explained what else he had learned from the French spy.

The voyage across the Atlantic had been terrible. Bonvouloir had never been happier to be back on land than when he reached Philadelphia, and he immediately made contact with Francis Daymon, whom he had met on his earlier travels. Francis Daymon had been born in France, himself, so Bonvouloir met with Daymon to plan the best way to proceed.

Julien Achard de Bonvouloir could not have imagined how fortunate this initial choice would become. Francis Daymon had immediate access to one of the most important men in the colonies— Benjamin Franklin.

Benjamin Franklin's eyes twinkled and there was a slight smile on his face, which had only smiled occasionally in the last several days. France was a traditional enemy of England. It was also a very strong country with an army and a navy that could truly help the American cause. France would make a splendid ally!

Forgetting his fear that Bonvouloir might be a double agent, Franklin was most interested in the prospects this French traveler offered.

"We must meet with this man," Franklin told Francis Daymon.

Then Benjamin Franklin quickly added, "But we must be very careful. If we are caught, there could be great consequences for all of us."

Francis did not think about the word "consequences." It was just the way Franklin spoke, making things sound important. Francis Daymon was happy that so far the effort he was making to help Julien Achard de Bonvouloir seemed to be working out so well.

Helping was exciting.

It was not until a few days later that Francis Daymon realized he would do more than help. The librarian was going to be closely involved in the meetings. He was becoming a spy for France and the colonists.

And the "consequences" which Franklin had mentioned could be death!

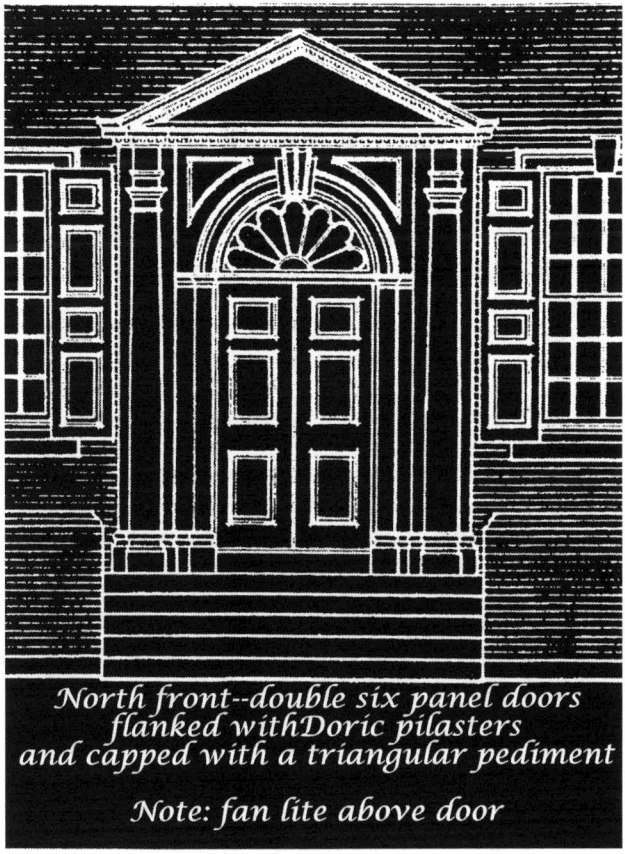

North front--double six panel doors
flanked with Doric pilasters
and capped with a triangular pediment

Note: fan lite above door

Front Doors

Behind the closed doors of Carpenters' Hall, Ben Franklin told Francis Daymon how dangerous it might be to meet with the mysterious stranger from France. He knew that once you go through some doors, you can never go back.

CHAPTER FOUR

'Tis easy to see, hard to foresee.

Poor Richard's Almanack
By Benjamin Franklin

*I*n the days that followed there was a great deal of preparation throughout the colonies. Most of the people in America were preparing to celebrate Christmas. A few were preparing for something else—something very frightening—a war with England.

Christmas in the colonies was a special time of fellowship and goodwill.

Children in the colonies no doubt were quite excited. Presents were left by Kris Kringle in their stockings, which they traditionally hung on the fireplace mantle Christmas Eve. These would be opened in the morning as well as other presents to mark the joyous occasion. Such presents were usually useful ones, such as food or clothing, and they were always appreciated, because in the years before the American Revolution people could not afford luxuries.

Much of what they owned were the necessities of their lives. Then the colonists would gather for morning services in the several churches throughout the city.

After church, everyone would return home or to the homes of family and friends for a large, delicious Christmas feast, which would include several meats, vegetables, potatoes, breads, and pastries, including mince pies and plum puddings, fruits, nuts, and candies.

Benjamin Franklin was a wonderful host at Christmas time. As many as two or three dozen guests would join him for Christmas dinner. There were refreshments and songs for the season; some were even composed by Franklin and played on the **glass harmonica**—a musical instrument he had invented. It was made of drinking glasses and played by running a wet finger around the rim of each glass.

But Benjamin Franklin's mood was mixed. He was happy for the joy of the Christmas season, but he was quite worried about the events that would surely take place in the New Year and especially those that would happen even sooner—the dangerous meetings he had arranged at Carpenters' Hall.

Ben Franklin surely wanted to be careful. He knew that the colonies did not have much hope of ever winning their independence, but if they were to have any chance at all, he would have to succeed in finding an ally. He would need Francis Daymon. He truly hated involving others. He was putting Francis Daymon in great danger, but Franklin could think of no other way.

"Noel, Noel!" he had heard the caroler sing, and his heart beat faster as he anticipated his future actions. For all the joy and goodwill this season should bring, there was no peace on earth in America this Christmas. Colonists in Massachusetts had already fought with English troops.

With all that was happening, Benjamin Franklin's thoughts were not on the Christmas porridge. He was thinking about all the danger that lay ahead. The tragedy and horrors of the war he knew could not be avoided. He thought of the lives of young Americans that would be lost—and then he also thought of Francis Daymon.

In the past few days his librarian had become indispensable to the success of the American Revolution. In fact, the opportunity to secure an ally for the American cause was not only made possible by Daymon, but the entire preparation for the communication during the meeting would be made through him.

In a way it made sense. There was some safety if they were caught together late at night. Francis Daymon and the Frenchman were friends, both having lived in France. Franklin was merely at the library doing some late-night research. If they were caught, it was possible, if they all told the same story, they could escape punishment. It was also possible they would all hang for **treason**. Benjamin Franklin worried about how he had involved Francis

Daymon deeply in this intrigue and espionage, but he realized he had no other choice.

Daymon was needed for a far more important reason than just arranging the meeting. Julien Achard de Bonvouloir did not speak English well, nor did Benjamin Franklin speak French well. If important communication was to take place between the two it would have to be with an interpreter, and Francis Daymon was, indeed, the only one in all Philadelphia whom Franklin could trust with that responsibility.

The librarian now knew how dangerous the mission was. He kept the embers in the fireplaces of Carpenters' Hall banked to provide as much heat as possible without giving out a flame to alert anyone working for the British government that someone was in the building past closing.

Georgian style Chimneypiece trimmed in wood

Chimneypiece

Georgian mantle and chimneypiece façade. There would be no fire, but also no children to hang their stockings from the Carpenters' Hall mantle. Still Ben Franklin was hoping for the best present ever.

The cold December night made Francis Daymon shiver— or maybe it was his own nervousness. He worried what would happen if, as interpreter, he used the wrong word. Someone might misunderstand, get angry, or leave because he had made a mistake. He was also nervous because he knew how critical Franklin now believed these meetings were.

"The entire hope for our future rests on our success," he had told Francis.

The success of the American Revolution for independence would be determined by what took place in these conversations. It was hard for Francis Daymon to understand how conversations could be so important, but Franklin had said these were extremely important. Daymon trusted Benjamin Franklin. His employer could see things that the librarian could not yet imagine.

Francis Daymon was now involved in international intrigue. That was the danger he was in—the "consequences" Benjamin Franklin had spoken about. If he was caught, he could be tried, convicted, and executed—as a spy.

British agents were everywhere. They could come to arrest him at any time. They could be walking up the front steps of Carpenters' Hall at any moment.

Francis Daymon was very nervous. He wanted to stoke the coals and warm the room with a fire, but he could not. Instead, he huddled closer to the embers and tried to warm himself while he waited. He tried not to think about the danger. He did not want to imagine what the British soldiers would do to him.

Then he heard footsteps outside.

CHAPTER FIVE

A slip of the foot you may soon recover, but a slip of the tongue you may never get over.

Poor Richard's Almanack
By Benjamin Franklin

*F*rancis Daymon waited as the footsteps stopped outside the front doors. If they were British soldiers come to arrest him there would be a very loud knock, maybe someone barking out for Daymon to give himself up, and then they would even smash in the doors. The double doors were very strong, but they would not keep out the soldiers of the King if they were determined to break them in and arrest Francis Daymon. He was thinking so hard about this that he almost did not hear the soft, quiet knock at the door.

It was not the British!

Daymon hurried to unlock the door. It must be either Bonvouloir, Franklin, or John Jay coming for their first secret meeting he thought. He did not want anyone waiting outside for fear someone sympathetic to the British might see him and figure something strange was happening at Carpenters' Hall.

Benjamin Franklin wanted John Jay included in these secret meetings. Jay was also a member of the Committee of Secret Correspondence, and he was much younger than Franklin, closer in age to Bonvouloir. Ben knew there were many advantages to having someone else negotiate with the French besides himself. His own years had given him experience and hopefully wisdom, but age had taken some stamina and youthful enthusiasm from him.

John Jay made an excellent partner in the secret negotiations. He had studied law and was a successful attorney. He was a representative from New York to the Continental Congress. One of the things that Benjamin Franklin admired most about Jay was that he could make a quick decision and stick by it if it was right, even if it was not a popular choice.

The instructions for all three men had been the same. Each was to approach Carpenters' Hall from a different part of the city, and none of them would take a direct route. They would arrive and leave at different times. Even Benjamin Franklin, who only lived about a block away, did not come directly to Carpenters' Hall.

Everything was going well. As each one arrived, they were certain they had not been followed. All was clear to proceed with the first meeting. Daymon went upstairs with Ben

Franklin, who had been the last to arrive. The librarian thought Franklin should be relieved that everything so far had gone as they had planned, but he had gotten to know his employer very well, and something was still bothering him. As they were climbing the stairs, Franklin stopped. Francis Daymon turned.

"There is still a reason we must be very careful of what we say in this first meeting," Franklin spoke softly to Francis Daymon. He went on to explain in a whisper, "If this man is a double agent, secretly working for the British, what we say may be delivered directly to our enemies. However, if this man is truly only working for France, but he turns out to be unwise or says something he shouldn't to someone else, then what we say may accidently fall into the hands of our enemies."

More and more, Francis Daymon was realizing how incredibly the odds were stacked against a successful ending to this act of espionage and intrigue.

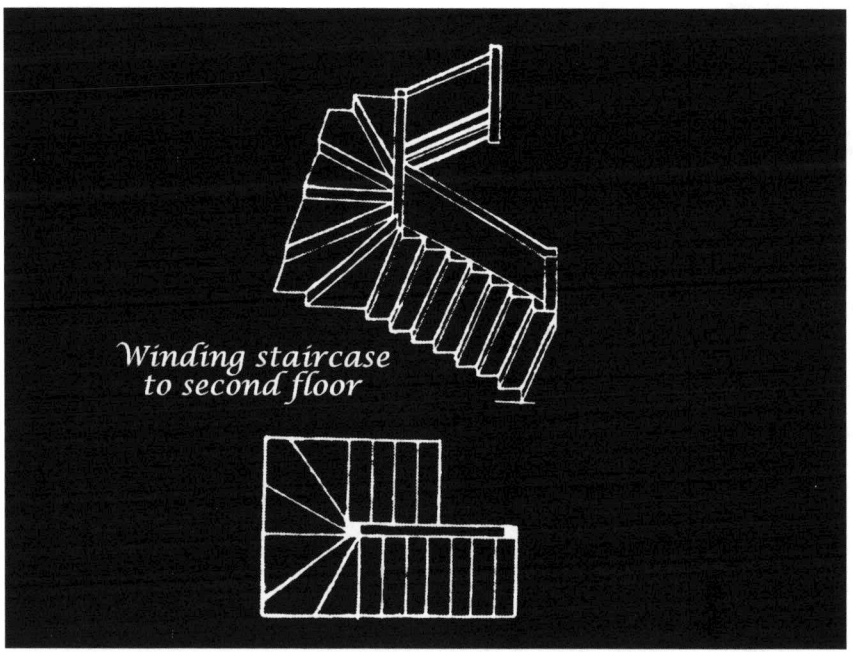

Winding Staircase

Ben Franklin appreciated the economic use of space in the winding staircase, but at his age he was cautious of twists and turns in his life.

They finished climbing the stairs to the second floor, and for a moment, in the dark, Francis Daymon had a fearful vision. He imagined himself climbing the steps of a scaffold beneath a hangman's noose.

He stumbled on the last step.

CHAPTER SIX

Wish not so much to live long as to live well.

Poor Richard's Almanack
By Benjamin Franklin

*I*t was cold that night in the second floor library of Carpenters' Hall, but Francis Daymon was perspiring as though it were summer. He was very nervous, and at first everything went quite slowly. He carefully translated each word Benjamin Franklin and John Jay said to Achard de Bonvouloir, and in turn he translated what the Frenchman said to the two Americans.

Soon, however, Francis Daymon was much more comfortable. He realized how easily he could perform what was needed, and the conversation between everyone flowed smoothly and quickly.

Still, this first gathering in the darkened library of Carpenters' Hall was a cautious one. Francis Daymon and Ben Franklin both realized that Chevalier Julien Alexandre Achard de Bonvouloir was not a double agent, for he was even more nervous than everyone else that he might be discovered and arrested. The terms of his commission from the King of France were quite definite. If he would be captured by the English, the French government would deny ever knowing hm or authorizing his mission.

Everyone spoke cautiously during this first meeting. As the hours moved by, it became quite obvious that the only real accomplishment was the parties achieved some degree of comfort with each other. It was resolved, therefore, to meet again to see if further progress and agreement could be made.

For two more nights in December, Benjamin Franklin and John Jay met with Achard de Bonvouloir. By necessity, Francis Daymon was there. Not only did he open the door for the individuals involved in this international intrigue, but he also made the actual communication possible. Daymon was the one who kept the talks moving forward by translating the discussion back and forth.

Eventually, Francis stopped thinking of the danger he and all the others were in, and the task of achieving an alliance with the French government became his overriding objective.

He became very concerned about ever achieving this goal. Bonvouloir was more than cautious. He would not commit to anything, but merely advised his American counterparts in this dangerous mission that he would report the needs of the colonies back to his associates in France.

Franklin and Jay tried to press for more commitment, but they were never successful in obtaining more than a desire on Bonvouloir's part to see what he could do for his new friends.

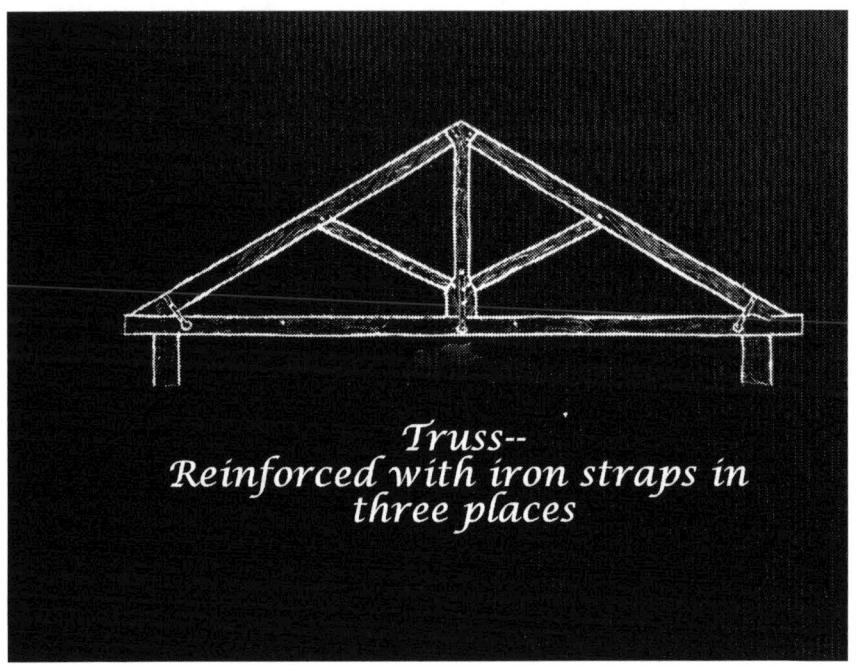

Truss--
Reinforced with iron straps in
three places

Truss

A **truss** is a triangle or series of triangles assembled together and used to hold up or support heavy loads, such as a roof. Franklin wondered if not France, what country could possibly support the colonies in a war against England?

When Bonvouloir pressed to commit the American colonies to a new **allegiance** with France rather than a mere alliance, Franklin and Jay were equally firm in making no agreements. In fact, Franklin made it quite clear that America would not trade one king for another. He had done this in an amusing but unmistakable fashion. He had a chessboard set up to play between himself and Bonvouloir before the third and final meeting.

As Bonvouloir sat, prepared to make his first move, Franklin reached over and removed both kings from the board. The shocked Frenchman looked at Francis Daymon for an explanation, but Daymon was equally bewildered.

Franklin, with a twinkle in his eye, whispered to Daymon to please explain to their French friend, "In America we have no need of kings."

Daymon explained this and many more things. John Jay and Benjamin Franklin pointed out that although Americans would never consent to a new allegiance to France to replace their domination by England, the alliance between the French and Americans would bring about markets and resources that France had so far been unable to gain. It could make France an equal to England in trade and commerce in the New World.

This was a significant objective and worth considering for the French government. As for the French King, there was the constant thorn of England, itself. Here was a chance to weaken his enemy and seek revenge for past losses in the previous war the French had fought with the English.

Through these three secret meetings, Francis Daymon carefully translated the words and expressions of all parties. By the end of the final meeting, he was not certain that any progress had been made. He then went downstairs and opened a door. Each left separately and stealthily so they were not noticed or followed. They went out into the dark night and an uncertain future filled with potential dangers.

When he had let the last of the three conspirators out the door, he locked it again and turned to the darkness of the first floor. For a moment he imagined he could hear once more the lively debates that Patrick Henry and Sam Adams and all the others had brought to this meeting place during the First Continental Congress. He remembered the cautious hope and faith so many of the colonists had had during those meetings. Now he had seen both John Jay's and Benjamin Franklin's faces filled with concern and perhaps disappointment. There had been no commitment made by the French government, itself. Perhaps America would be left on its own in its struggle against the most powerful nation on earth.

Had he, Francis Daymon, risked his life for nothing? Had these three dangerous meetings been worthless? Had all his efforts been a failure?

CHAPTER SEVEN

Little strokes fell great oaks.

Poor Richard's Almanack
By Benjamin Franklin

*I*n the days that followed, Francis Daymon learned that his employer's serious expression was not due to a belief that the meetings with Bonvouloir were a failure.

Ben Franklin was standing in the first floor of Carpenters' Hall with the sun shining brightly through the **fan lite window** above the back door, "Quite the contrary," he told Daymon. "I believe we have made great progress."

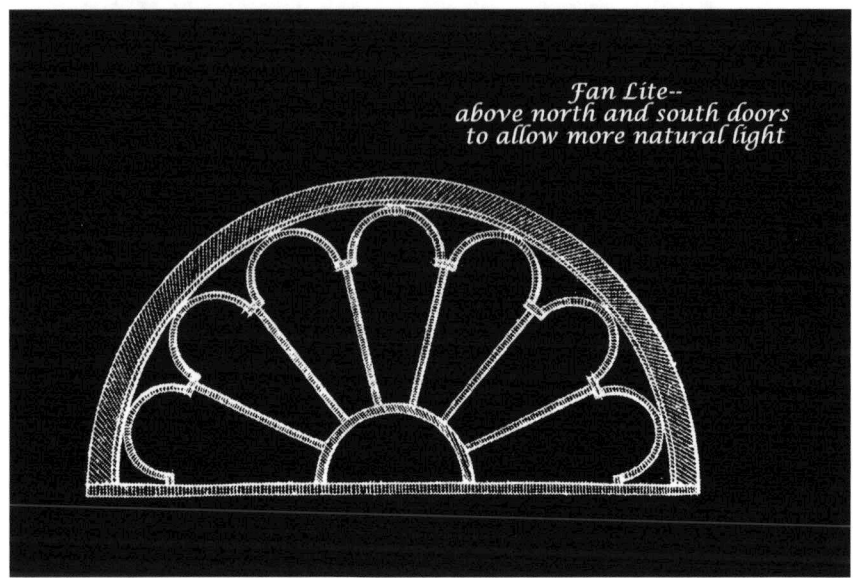

Fan Lite

Even though it was afternoon, the sun light through the fan lite window reminded Franklin of a sunrise and it cheered his spirits to think of the dawn of a new and wonderful day.

Benjamin Franklin explained to Francis that, just as it took plans to construct Carpenters' Hall, preparing for a successful revolution required plans. Careful planning would prove to be well worth their time as the revolution unfolded in the coming months.

In essence, Franklin was creating what others might term a "**blueprint**" for a revolution. He looked at Carpenters' Hall, and he spoke again to Daymon. "With a plan and careful attention to details we might someday build something even more beautiful than this building. We might build the nation men and women have left their homeland for—a nation founded on freedom for all, and one built to last forever."

The reason why he had been so somber, Franklin explained, was that he foresaw ever more clearly the terror and horror of the war that would be fought with England. It was a time in which friends and neighbors would be torn apart. The future of the freedom movement in America depended on enough good men and women willing to sacrifice and pay the price for the generations to come.

For his part, Bonvouloir had agreed to write a very important report on the state of the American colonies. Through Achard de Bonvouloir, the French King and his ministers would learn that the revolutionary movement in the American colonies was genuine and backed by some of the most important and influential people in the New World. He also would report that the possibility of the colonists succeeding in their revolution was not certain, but that they did possess the desire and determination to ultimately secure their independence.

This point alone would prompt the French King to secretly send weapons and **munitions** to the colonists so they could fight against the well-trained British army and navy.

Francis Daymon could not know this in the days after the secret meetings, but it was the report that Bonvouloir would deliver to the French King that ultimately secured the invitation for Benjamin Franklin to travel to Paris after the revolution began.

Had Francis Daymon never arranged the meetings between Achard de Bonvouloir and the two American conspirators—John Jay and Benjamin Franklin—and had he not been able to translate for the conspirators in the upper room of Carpenters' Hall, the journey of Benjamin Franklin to France would probably never have taken place.

It was while Franklin was in Paris that he was able to convince the French to join as allies in the American revolutionary cause. The alliance with France was crucial, and without that great nation's help, the American colonists could not have defeated the British forces. The French King sent soldiers to America. More importantly, he sent the French fleet that enabled George Washington to trap the British General Cornwallis in Yorktown, forcing the surrender of the English army. This surrender ended the American Revolutionary War. The colonists were victorious, and shortly afterward the United States of America would be founded.

All these things Francis Daymon could not have realized. He did not even understand how important a part he had played in the history of America, but without him, there possibly would not be a United States of America.

The name Francis Daymon is not one highlighted in the history books, but had he not done his part, the efforts of others could never have succeeded. Daymon was one of many men and women who have contributed to the great story that is known throughout the world as America. It is an unfinished story, and truly an imperfect one. However, as long as men and women continue to do their part, as Francis Daymon did his when he had the opportunity, the American story, and the American cause of liberty and freedom for all will never end.

GLOSSARY

Allegiance A promise to a larger group to do what is right, such as when someone "...pledges allegiance to the flag and to the Republic for which it stands..."

Alliance The joining of two or more people, groups, or countries.

Ally Someone who will help you when you are in need.

Bifocal Glasses Invented by Benjamin Franklin, the top half of each lens helps the viewer see distant objects while the bottom half helps the person see closer objects.

Blueprint Years ago a blueprint was a plan drawn in white on blue paper showing builders what was to be built. Builders now use computer printouts and not blueprints. Today the word "blueprint" means a plan of how to make something happen.

Cupola A small dome on top of a roof. *Note: In the photograph of the Cupola on Carpenters' Hall there is also a **weather vane** and a **lightning rod**.*

Cupola

Daylight Savings The practice of moving clocks ahead by one hour during the summer months so that daylight lasts longer at night. It is meant to save energy. In colonial times they would not have to burn candles until much later at night.

Dentil Small square or rectangular blocks that are placed below other wood molding as decoration. Some think they look like teeth.

Dentil

Doric Pilaster

Doric Pilaster A column, often sticking out from a wall and capped by a block, which can also have other decorative molding. *In Photograph Doric Pilasters are on both sides of the front door.*

Fan lite Window (or Fanlight) A half circle window over a door or another window. *(See photo above of front door with Doric pilasters and fan lite, as well as fanlight above southern doors)*

Fan Lite

Flemish Bond Bricks placed in a wall so that there is an alternate pattern on the outside between short (header) and long (stretcher) sides of the brick.

Franklin Stove A cast iron, free-standing fireplace designed by Benjamin Franklin and Robert Grace that used less fuel to burn while giving off more heat into the room.

Gabled Ends The triangular part of a wall where two sloped sections of roof meet.

Gabled End

Georgian Architecture A period of building in English countries during the reigns of Kings George I through George IV (1714 – 1830). Usually brick constructions, the designs are characterized by symmetry and balance.

Georgian Mantle A ledge above the opening of a fireplace that is supported by carved supports and some fancy details.

Georgian Mantle

Glass Harmonica A series of glass bowls that when touched on the top edge with a wet finger makes a musical tone—each a different note due to the size of the bowl.

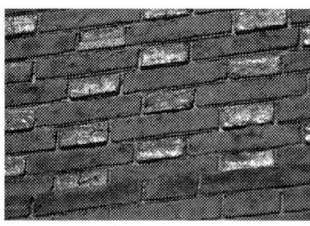
Glazed Header

Glazed Header The shorter end of a brick that has been left closest to the kiln's opening so that it receives more oxygen and "burning" to make it shiny black.

Greek Cross Plan A cross in which all four arms are of equal length.

Gulf Stream A warm current that flows along the eastern coast of the United States starting in the Gulf of Mexico.

Lightning Rod A metal stake attached to the top of a building so lightning will strike it rather than the building, itself. The electric charge is carried safely to the ground through a wire. *See Cupola for picture.*

Munitions Materials used in war, such as ammunition.

Pediment A triangular design placed above a door or window.

Pediment

Plan View Looking down at a building's shape from above without a roof

Stretcher It is the long side of the brick.

Treason The crime of betraying one's country.

Stretcher

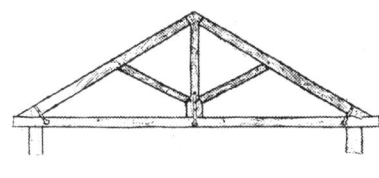
Truss

Truss A triangle or series of triangles used to support a roof, bridge, or some other heavy load.

"Which way the wind blows" This is an expression known as an idiom in which a wise person is reminded of simple truths. For example, a farmer might be able to tell a change in weather by knowing which way the wind blows. In colonial days sailors needed to know the direction of the wind to help sail their boat.

Weathervane An instrument put on the highest point of a building. It turns as the wind moves it, showing which direction the wind is blowing.

Carpenters' Hall

Carpenters' Hall Today
Carpenters' Hall is open to the public free of charge. For more
information about the building, its history, and hours of operation
visit **www.carpentershall.org**

The Carpenters' Company was founded in 1724, and its members have always been leaders of the construction industry, as well as contributors to the development of the city, region and nation. The present membership of the Company, in addition to carrying on the tradition of industry and community leadership, are privileged to maintain the priceless historic treasure, Carpenters' Hall.

ABOUT THE AUTHORS

Charles and Nancy Cook are enjoying their fourth decade of marriage. The Spies at Carpenters' Hall represents a different type of collaboration by the couple. With extensive experience in elementary education, Nancy has helped Charlie write an important story for children about a critical moment in American history, and how each child should grow up knowing that the efforts of each and every person can make a difference. Charles is a member of the Carpenters' Company that maintains Carpenters' Hall. Due to its historical significance, in 1851 Carpenters' Hall was the first privately held building in America opened to the public, and it remains so today free of charge. Spanning a career in construction of over fifty years, Charles now teaches Construction Management at Drexel University. In 2019 he received the Educator of the Year Award by the Associated General Contractors of America for his ability to bring engaging lessons to both his Face to Face and On-line students.

Charles and Nancy continue to enjoy time spent with their friends and family living in suburban Philadelphia.

Printed in the United States
By Bookmasters